MY MAMA SAYS
THERE AREN'T ANY
ZOMBIES, GHOSTS, VAMPIRES,
CREATURES, DEMONS, MONSTERS,
FIENDS, GOBLINS, OR THINGS

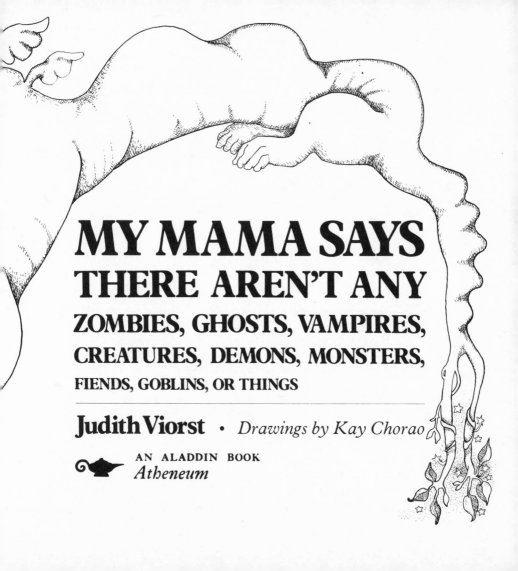

MY MAMA SAYS
THERE AREN'T ANY
ZOMBIES, GHOSTS, VAMPIRES,
CREATURES, DEMONS, MONSTERS,
FIENDS, GOBLINS, OR THINGS

Judith Viorst • *Drawings by Kay Chorao*

AN ALADDIN BOOK
Atheneum

PUBLISHED BY ATHENEUM
TEXT COPYRIGHT © 1973 BY JUDITH VIORST
ILLUSTRATIONS COPYRIGHT © 1973 BY KAY SPROAT CHORAO
ALL RIGHTS RESERVED
PUBLISHED SIMULTANEOUSLY IN CANADA BY
MC CLELLAND & STEWART, LTD.
MANUFACTURED IN THE UNITED STATES OF AMERICA BY
CONNECTICUT PRINTERS, HARTFORD
ISBN 0-689-70439-9

To my very own Nick,
who helped me write this book.

My mama says there isn't any mean-eyed monster
with long slimy hair and pointy claws
going scritchy-scratch, scritchy-scritchy-scratch
outside my window.

But yesterday my mama said
I couldn't have some cream cheese on my sandwich,
because, she said, there wasn't any more.

And then I found the cream cheese

under the lettuce

in back of the Jello. So…

sometimes even mamas make mistakes.

My mama says that a vampire
isn't flying over my house
with his red and black vampire cape
and his vampire f-f-f-fangs.

But how can I believe her

when she said my wriggly tooth would fall out Thursday,

and then it stayed till Sunday after lunch?

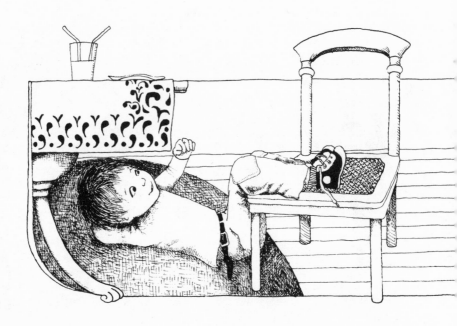

And once she gave me 19 cents
when yo-yos cost a quarter. So...
sometimes even mamas make mistakes.

On certain nights

when everyone's cozy and sleeping,

all of a sudden I hear a Thing in the yard.

And you know what it says as it ooooozes along?

It says, Nick, I am coming to get you.

mama says it's positively not.

But when we shopped at the supermarket Friday,
my mama told me to carry the bag with the eggs.
It's heavy, I said, too heavy for me.
Oh, you can do it, she told me.

I can't.

You can.

I can't.

You can.

I can't.

You can, she told me.

And that's how there got to be scrambled eggs
all over my shoes.

And that lady. So...

sometimes even mamas make mistakes.

And sometimes in my bunk bed I start thinking,
maybe a fiend sneaked into my lower bunk.
And he's sniffing around for a boy to eat,
and I'm the boy that he's sniffing, and…
My mama says no fiends have sneaked in here.

But why did she scold me for leaving my skates

on the sidewalk?

Those were Anthony's skates.

I remembered to put mine away.

And once she said I hadn't flushed,

and it was Alexander's. So…

sometimes even mamas make mistakes.

My mama says that a tall white ghost
who goes "hoo!" from a hole in its mouth,
isn't hoo-hoo-hooing in my closet.

This morning, though, she made me wear my boots.
And then it didn't rain—or even drizzle.

And once I asked for chocolate nut
and she brought back rum raisin. So...
sometimes even mamas make mistakes.

My mama says that a zombi

with his eyes rolled back in his head,

and his arms out stiff,

and his skin as cold as ice,

isn't clonking up and up the stairs.

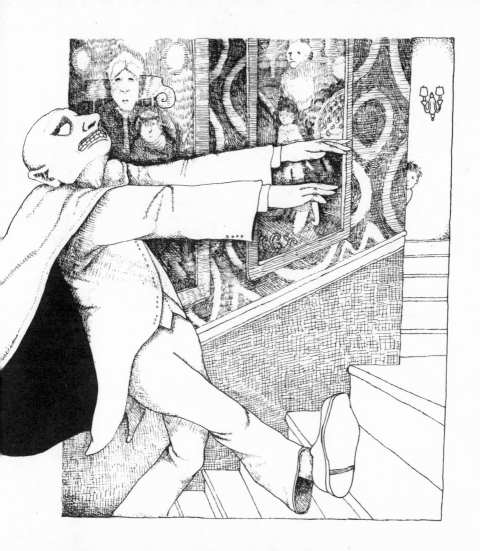

But how can I believe her

when she told me Holly's middle name was Susan.

And Holly's middle name is really Jane.

And once she said I wasn't

when I told her I was going to be car sick. So...

sometimes even mamas make mistakes.

And sometimes in the dark a demon

is switching his spidery tail.

And waiting.

Waiting for someone.

Who could it be?

And he's laughing a "heh!"

And a "hah!"

And a "hee!"

Which could give someone goose bumps in summer.

He isn't there, my mama says to me.

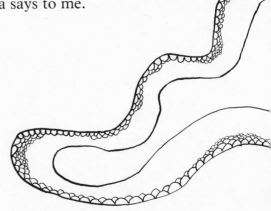

But how does she know

when she still doesn't know how to drive me

to Christopher's house without getting us lost on the way?

She tells me, Zip your jacket up.

But she can't zip it either. So...

sometimes even mamas make mistakes.

And I'm sure I've seen a goblin
slinking out of my dresser drawer
with a sack on his back to take me to goblin-y lands
where boys and girls eat brussels sprouts
and never get a birthday.
Oh, no, you haven't, Mama always says.

But Monday Mama said
she put my crayons on my shelf.
Just use your eyes, she said,
and you will find them.
I can't.
You can.
I can't.
You can.
I can't.

All right! *I'll* find them,
she said (not very nicely).
But, guess what?
She couldn't, too. So...
sometimes even mamas make mistakes.

My mama says that a creature

isn't reaching out his hand

to pinch me,

or squinch me,

or push me,

or squush me,

or—agggh!

Well, sometimes even mamas make mistakes.

But sometimes they don't.

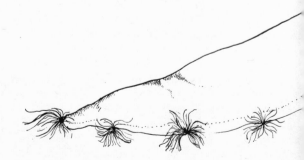

Judith Viorst has been writing for the more than ten years that she has been married, with a lot of helpful encouragement from her husband and three sons. She loves children's books and tries to write books that her own children will like—and in which they will sometimes recognize themselves. Her husband is also a free-lance writer, and he works at home as she does. As one of their children once explained, "My father is a typewriter, and I think my mother is too." Among her books for children are *The Tenth Good Thing About Barney* and *Alexander and the Terrible, Horrible, No Good, Very Bad Day.*

Kay Chorao lives in New York City with her husband, Ernesto, and their three sons, Jamie, Peter and Ian. She graduated from Wheaton College in Massachusetts and did graduate study at The Chelsea School of Art in London, England. She is the author-illustrator of *The Repair of Uncle Toe* and *A Magic Eye for Ida.*

Deck the halls with boughs of holly.
Fa-la-la-la-la, la-la-la-la
'Tis the season to be jolly.
Fa-la-la-la-la, la-la-la-la
Don we now our gay apparel.
Fa-la-la-la-la, la-la-la-la
Troll the ancient Yule-tide carol.
Fa-la-la-la-la, la-la-la-la

See the blazing Yule before us.
Fa-la-la-la-la, la-la-la-la
Strike the harp and join the chorus.
Fa-la-la-la-la, la-la-la-la
Follow me in merry measure.
Fa-la-la-la-la, la-la-la-la
While I tell of Yule-tide treasure.
Fa-la-la-la-la, la-la-la-la

Fast away the old year passes.
Fa-la-la-la-la, la-la-la-la
Hail the new year, lads and lasses.
Fa-la-la-la-la, la-la-la-la
Sing we joyous, all together.
Fa-la-la-la-la, la-la-la-la
Heedless of the wind and weather.
Fa-la-la-la-la, la-la-la-la

CHRIS MOUSE
and the Christmas House

by Deanna Luke

Illustrated by JoAnn A. Woytek

Blessing Our World, Inc.
Palestine, Texas 75802-0642

Chris Mouse Dedication

I want to dedicate Chris Mouse and the Christmas House to my parents,
S.J. and Inez Anderson. My imagination was given wonderful space when
I was a child and their continued belief in me encourages me to share
stories with audiences of all ages. I also want to dedicate this to our
grandchildren, Nicole, Miles, Susannah, and Timothy. They are my
favorite audience and most delightful critics. I love them all.

Special Thanks

My husband, Jerry's belief in me is indeed a gift I am thankful for
daily. I am also thankful to the Lord for the ideas that seed stories
like Chris Mouse and the Christmas House. Our illustrator, JoAnn Woytek
is a joy to work with as she translates my words into pictures.

Dedication from JoAnn A. Woytek

To God be the Glory through Jesus. I praise His Holy name.
I thank Him for my loving husband and precious children.

First Edition.   10 9 8 7 6 5 4 3 2 1

Copyright 2001 Blessing Our World, Inc.

Text © 1981, 1998, 2000 Deanna Luke

Illustrations © 1998 Blessing Our World, Inc.

Illustrations are water color style using permanent acrylic inks.

Book design by Janet Long.

Body copy typeface is Benguiat Gothic Bold. Title type face is Gill Sans Extra Bold.

Publisher's Cataloging-in-Publication Data Prepared by Blessing Our World, Inc.

Luke, Deanna, 1948–

Chris Mouse and the Christmas House / by Deanna Luke; illustrated by JoAnn A. Woytek.

Summary: A story of a mouse and a wonderful life, curiosity, and the lesson he learned.

LCCN 00-190709   ISBN 1-928777-04-X

[1. Picture Books for Children 2. Prose and Children]   I. Woytek, JoAnn A., Ill.   IL Title

Printed in South Korea

SAN 299-8920

Blessing Our World, Inc.
P.O. Box 642
Palestine, Texas 75802-0642 USA
Phone 1-903-729-1129

CHRIS MOUSE
and the Christmas House

Once there was a Christmas House,
And in it lived our friend, Chris Mouse.

Every day was Christmas in the Christmas House
So, every day was Christmas, for our friend, Chris Mouse.

The songs of Christmas played.
The sights of Christmas stayed.
And...Oh, the wonderful
smells of Christmas,
Everywhere were made.

Chris Mouse could go
from room to room
To see each decoration.
The lights, the baubles,
and icicles, too—
All a fine creation.

There were trees
    in every room,
One of green and red,
One of silver,
    and of gold;
"Beautiful!"
    Chris Mouse said.

At morning he awakened
To "Deck the Halls," playing all about.
Shoppers would come from close at hand,
And others from further out.

Because he had never
lived anywhere else,
Chris thought all houses
were like his own,
With trees and lights,
with music and gifts,
And candles, all that shone.

People loved the Christmas House,
And came from far and near.
As they came their voices were full of cheer,
Exclaiming, "Come here, Come here!"

Chris Mouse saw the ladies of the Christmas House
Leave every single night,
And then Chris would climb the highest tree,
Up to the highest height.

The ladies returned again each day
With the morning bright,
And in their hands were toys and trees—
Boy, they looked a sight!

Chris Mouse would hear the key in the lock
And scurry to his hiding place.
The ladies would talk as they moved things around
To make some extra space.

He would hear people talking
of a day close at hand.
Hurry, hustle, bustle,
they would come and go.
Yet the Christmas House
so glorious and grand
Seemed to Chris Mouse
to be the same and so...

Chris Mouse wanted to go home with someone
To see what day she would celebrate.
He thought he was missing something fabulous and fine,
And didn't want to wait.

So...on the morning of Christmas Eve
Chris Mouse came up with a plan.
He would tuck himself into a gift
And leave in a customer's van.

As the ladies selected a vase to wrap,
Chris Mouse made his move.
He scurried into the box for that gift,
Right down to the bottom groove.

Carols played as the ladies wrapped
This gift for the special day.
Chris Mouse waited in his hiding place,
And knew he would be okay.
He had only heard about Christmas,
But now he would surely see!
For then the door opened and a lady said,
"Oh, this must be for me!"

It was the lady to pick up the gift,
She said it was her last.
He knew he was about to see
What he had only heard of in the past.

Chris Mouse held on for dear life.
He was in the box she put on the floor.
There was no music playing now,
No busy opening and closing door.

Once the room had gotten quiet
He almost gave a great big shout.
Where were the sounds, the smells,
And the people coming in and out?

The Christmas House hummed
throughout Christmas Eve,
From morning until twilight came.
As one Lady locked up the store,
She said "I think it's such a shame…

For weeks and weeks of effort,
Spent for just one day,
When we know that the Spirit of Christmas
Is meant for the whole year to stay."

Chris finally decided he wanted to see
What he had heard of in the Christmas House.
He nibbled all night right through tissue and wrap
Until out sprang one very full Chris Mouse.

He found himself beneath a tree
Just like the ones in the store.
He couldn't see anything different
Than where he had been before.

He waited 'til morning
    for the lady of the house
And her family on Christmas Day.
At dawn they ran into the room
And the little ones led the way.

They picked up gifts
    and opened them,
And then they hugged each other.
Chris Mouse was glad
    he'd come to see this
And wished for his own brother.

Just when things were going great,
The family left the room.
In their pathway, they had left
All the paper strewn.

They had gone in another room,
Where no mess had been made.
There he found the family,
As they read and sang and played.

After eating a meal fit for a king,
The family quieted down.
No more celebration, no carols played.
Chris realized this with a frown.

The day after Christmas,
    Chris Mouse sadly saw
The decorations disappear.
"Now I know the truth," he thought,
And Chris Mouse shed a tear.

"How will I ever in a million years
Get back to the Christmas House?
I made a horrible, terrible mistake,"
Said one very sad Chris Mouse.

At breakfast he heard the lady say,
"Guess where there's a half-price sale?
The Christmas House—I have to go!"
And Chris knew all would be well.

He went out of the house,
To get in the van and be ready for the ride.
He knew if he ever, ever got back,
The Christmas House was where he'd reside.

Sure enough the lady came out
And quickly started the van.
Chris Mouse knew with excitement
This would be his last big plan.

When they reached the Christmas House
Chris jumped out the van door;
And followed the lady and others
As they were going into the store.

Chris Mouse had had his fill
Of people and of places.
He could not wait to see the sweet
Christmas ladies' faces.

The people talked, the music played,
Lights were just a-twinkling.
The smells of Christmas were everywhere,
Outside the snow was sprinkling.

The ladies had left him cookies
And some cheese they called Swiss Lace.
Chris Mouse sat down to nibble them
In his own special place.

Christmas music met him
And welcomed Chris Mouse home.
Now that he was safely back,
He vowed to never roam.

Chris Mouse had learned a lesson,
One he would not forget.
The Christmas House
   was perfect for him
For it was Christmas yet!

Deck the halls with boughs of holly.
Fa-la-la-la-la, la-la-la-la
'Tis the season to be jolly.
Fa-la-la-la-la, la-la-la-la
Don we now our gay apparel.
Fa-la-la-la-la, la-la-la-la
Troll the ancient Yule-tide carol.
Fa-la-la-la-la, la-la-la-la

See the blazing Yule before us.
Fa-la-la-la-la, la-la-la-la
Strike the harp and join the chorus.
Fa-la-la-la-la, la-la-la-la
Follow me in merry measure.
Fa-la-la-la-la, la-la-la-la
While I tell of Yule-tide treasure.
Fa-la-la-la-la, la-la-la-la

Fast away the old year passes.
Fa-la-la-la-la, la-la-la-la
Hail the new year, lads and lasses.
Fa-la-la-la-la, la-la-la-la
Sing we joyous, all together.
Fa-la-la-la-la, la-la-la-la
Heedless of the wind and weather.
Fa-la-la-la-la, la-la-la-la